THE OTHER ONE

A HEART WRENCHING STORY

PRIYANKA PUJA

Copyright © Priyanka Puja
All Rights Reserved.

This book has been self-published with all reasonable efforts taken to make the material error-free by the author. No part of this book shall be used, reproduced in any manner whatsoever without written permission from the author, except in the case of brief quotations embodied in critical articles and reviews.

The Author of this book is solely responsible and liable for its content including but not limited to the views, representations, descriptions, statements, information, opinions and references ["Content"]. The Content of this book shall not constitute or be construed or deemed to reflect the opinion or expression of the Publisher or Editor. Neither the Publisher nor Editor endorse or approve the Content of this book or guarantee the reliability, accuracy or completeness of the Content published herein and do not make any representations or warranties of any kind, express or implied, including but not limited to the implied warranties of merchantability, fitness for a particular purpose. The Publisher and Editor shall not be liable whatsoever for any errors, omissions, whether such errors or omissions result from negligence, accident, or any other cause or claims for loss or damages of any kind, including without limitation, indirect or consequential loss or damage arising out of use, inability to use, or about the reliability, accuracy or sufficiency of the information contained in this book.

Made with ♥ on the Notion Press Platform
www.notionpress.com

I dedicate this book to the person who NEVER gets tired of inspiring me

I LOVE YOU, MA

Contents

Foreword

Many girls are getting sexually abused since childhood without realising that they are being wronged. Most unfortunately, they fall victims to very near and dear ones like uncles, cousins. They have to keep their mouths shut to maintain their family's reputation unscathed. In this process, they start blaming themselves for what happened. Our main character in this story Nanda, is no different. She has been abused since childhood. Being deprived of parental affection, she hopes to find a sympathetic partner in her husband, Kamal. But Kamal's mysterious nature fails to give her mental peace. She has to face the same nightmares like her childhood. She has lost her mental balance. For her recovery, she needs mental support. She needs to feel safe. Only true love and affection can heal her wounded mind.

CHAPTER ONE

Nanda

Nanda`s eyes shoot open. She holds her breath, straining her ears in the darkness of her bedroom. She can hear a faint sound. Her husband Kamal is sleeping just beside her. The moonlight streams through the sheer window curtain and Nanda can see Kamal's peaceful and innocent face. Everything is quiet around and nothing suspicious draws Nanda's attention." I must be dreaming!"- she murmurs and falls back to sleep only to wake up hearing the sound again.

Her sleep breaks completely and she jolts up on bed. This time the sound appears louder and creepier as if someone is in the kitchen just beside the bedroom. Her heart pounds as she carefully slides out from under the sheets, trying not to make a sound. Nanda creeps across the room and feels along the wall for the stick that Kamal keeps near the door. Kamal is still beside her in deep sleep.

" It can't be a dream!! Someone must have broken into our house. Who can be it- a thief? a refugee seeking shelter? or maybe it's just a mouse? I may be thinking too much!!" Nanda tries to calm herself.

Gripping the stick tightly, she inches towards the kitchen. Another muffled noise makes her freeze in her tracks. It sounds like someone - or something - is rummaging around kitchen.

Nanda's mind races. She has been living here with her husband Kamal peacefully. Her neighbourhood is quiet and feels safe, but anything can happen in the middle of the night. What if it is an intruder? What if they have a weapon?

She stays absolutely still, listening. More shuffling and a faint metallic clank. Coming from the kitchen for sure. She begins creeping down the steps, one by one, her heart thundering against her ribs.

She gathers all her courage and tiptoes towards the kitchen. Nothing seems disturbed. But when she turns toward the kitchen doorway, though it is quite dark, she can see the silhouette of the stranger. Moonlight coming from the window is enough for Nanda to see the stranger standing near the stove. A tall, thin male wearing a white sleeping suit is looking out the window, holding a cup with both hands. Nanda finds a striking resemblance between the stranger and Kamal.

'Kamal has a similar strange way of holding a cup. But it can't be him! If Kamal is standing right here, who is lying on the bed!! Is she still dreaming?'-These thoughts send chills down Nanda's spine and she screams out of fear.

That stranger turns around but his face is still not clear enough. He speaks in a very soft voice. "Arre Nanda, it's me! Why are you shouting in middle of night? I couldn't sleep, so made some coffee. Did l scare you? Oh dear! It's my fault. " He proceeds towards Nanda stretching arms."Please come to me, dear! My Nandu darling please don't be scared! Come to me." - he tries to convince her. As he inches towards Nanda, slowly his face becomes distinct.

'Yes, it is Kamal! Kamal calls her 'Nandu darling' affectionately. That stranger is none other than Kamal! But who is lying on the bed then?' Nanda cringes in fear. She turns her head towards the bedroom expecting none on the bed but to her utter shock, she still sees the other 'Kamal' sleeping on the bed! Nanda can't bear the shock and falls down on the floor and collapses immediately.

Around 3 AM in the morning, Kamal suddenly wakes up to some muffled crying sound coming from the washroom. He shifts to the side of the bed to check on Nanda. But she is not there by his side. Kamal can still hear the sound coming from the washroom as if someone is crying and whimpering. Worry takes over Kamal thinking that Nanda must be in some trouble. He rushes towards the washroom and opens the door slowly. Nanda is sitting on the floor. Her hair is wet and her body is shaking continuously. Kamal tries to scoop Nanda in his arms but she shrugs off.

"No..No..don't come to me. Don't touch me. You are not him. You are the other one. Go away. No..No..don't come, don't touch ." Nanda is repeating the same words again and again as if she is hallucinating. As if she can't recognise Kamal. Her face turns completely pale and shivering continues. Kamal carries her outside the washroom forcefully and lay her on the bed. He tries to bring her back to reality but no luck. Nanda keeps talking gibberish and finally loses her sense.

The nextdoor neighbour Damini comes to Kamal's rescue when he knocks at their door. She changes Nanda's wet clothes and wraps a warm blanket around her. Damini makes hot soup for Nanda and tries to put some in her mouth but fails as Nanda shuts her mouth tightly. It is important to bring Nanda's consciousness first.

Damini has been in neighbourhood for more than a year. She has known Kamal as very aloof and unsocial. Whenever she tries to make a conversation with him, Kamal pulls away. After Kamal and Nanda's marriage there has been no celebration. The couple has been living a secluded secret life.

Damini's effort to make a bond with Nanda has been a failure. Damini has not seen Nanda last few months until today's bizzare circumstances. Looking at Nanda's condition many questions are rising in Damini's mind. Though Nanda`s eyes are closed, she is continuously blabbering 'It's not him. It's not Kamal. Tell him to go away! Don't let him to touch me. He is the 'Devil'. Go away! Go away!'

'Is she dreaming or she is really afraid of something or someone? Has Kamal done something wrong to her or Nanda is just being paranoid?' Damini is trying to find answers.

Nanda feels water sprinkling on her face and can hear a faint voice from afar calling her name, "Nanda, Nanda wake up! Can you hear me? Nanda! Follow my voice. Wake up Nanda. Open your eyes!"

Nanda opens her eyes very slowly. Her body starts shaking from fever. She has already lost the strength to sit up. Through her blurry vision, she only makes out the worrisome face of Kamal. Kamal is trying to comfort her. But Nanda is still in shock. She is yet to come out of the nightmare she has had.

CHAPTER TWO

Dr.Ranjan`s Chamber

Kamal is sitting at a famous psychiatric Dr. Ranjan's clinic. He has been at first hesitant to take an appointment from a psychiatrist. His middle-class sentiment has been stopping him from seeking help for his wife Nanda's mental issues. But whatever has been happening since his marriage with Nanda, has put him in such a situation that he is now compelled to look for someone who can help Nanda dealing with mental issues.

Since that night Nanda had been behaving very weird especially when Kamal is around her. She refuses to be anywhere close to Kamal. If Kamal ever has tried to come close to her, Nanda has become hysterical. She cries and screams loudly. Maximum times she closes herself inside the bedroom and waits for Kamal's departure. She keeps saying "I know you are not my husband Kamal. You are 'the other one'. What do you want from me? Where did you hide my husband? No, no, don't touch! Don't even try to come close! I will tell everyone your secret. You are not Kamal!"

Kamal has underestimated the situation at the beginning. He has considered it just a phase which will fade away soon. Perhaps, Nanda is taking more time to come out of the shock. He has convinced himself with this thought.

He has been trying to calm Nanda down in many ways but has failed miserably.

Nanda has been getting more violent day by day. With time Nanda's health condition is getting worse. Surprisingly Nanda is behaving absolutely normal when Kamal is not around her. Kamal's presence brings some unknown fear in Nanda's mind and that can be clearly observed in her behaviour.

Giving up all hope, a devastated Kamal has made up his mind to see psychiatrist Dr.Ranjan. Dr.Ranjan is a famous name in his field. Numerous certificates, degrees have been showcased all around his chamber. Uncountable success stories in curing various kinds of mental diseases are on display in front of Kamal's eyes. He is Kamal's last hope for Nanda's recovery. If Dr.Ranjan can cure Nanda, Kamal can get back to his happy and peaceful life with her.

Kamal is waiting for his turn while many questions keep popping up in his mind. 'Will Nanda become normal again? Can she ever get over the shock? Will this doctor be able to help Nanda? Most importantly will Dr. Ranjan believe even a word of what I am going to say!!?` Kamal has been thinking over and over but has failed to find a proper answer to any of his queries. Suddenly someone announces Kamal's name as next appointee at the doctor's chamber, breaking his stupor. He rises to his shaky feet and inches towards the chamber with a mixed feelings of hope and fear.

CHAPTER THREE

Dr.Ranjan

Human mind is my obsession. I try to understand its depth, the layers within layers. Mental health has been neglected for years ignoring the fact that how powerful a mind can be! How a sickness can spread from mind to body. Our subconscious has all the answers to our queries. Just we have to dig deep. We have to reach the subconscious.

All secrets lie in there. Patients with different types of mental sickness visit my chamber consuming my whole day. Yes, I dedicate all of my time to my profession to fill the well of loneliness inside me. My ex-wife Labanya is my first love. We met in friends' gathering and chemistry sparked between us. From romancing to getting married was quite smooth for us.

The day we invited little Kuhu into our lives, I was reborn with overwhelming love, affection as a father. I still can see those happy moments closing my eyes which lasted only for a few years. As days passed, I was excelling in my field. I had to visit clinics, chambers and attend numerous conferences all together.

Occasions like our marriage anniversary, Kuhu's birthday, her annual function day at school all took a back seat. My flourished professional life and passion about 'Human Psychology' took a toll on my family. I could spend less time with Labanya and Kuhu. Our house was getting bigger as well as space between us. Labanya had been trying to adjust with my busy lifestyle but one day her patience reached the limit. It was Kuhu's 10th birthday and arrangements were going on for a full- fledged celebration.

I rescheduled all my appointments on that particular day just to make it very special for Kuhu. I hatched a plan for vacation with my family long pending just after the celebration. I wanted to spend quality time curtailing distance among us. Finally that day arrived. All arrangements were done. Kuhu was about to cut the cake around 8 PM. So I was preparing to leave my chamber by 7 PM.

The moment I was about to drive back home, I received an urgent call from one of my patients, Ms.Malini. She had a husband but they had been living separate lives. Her only daughter was staying in boarding school. Malini was undergoing severe depression after her separation from husband and only child. On call she sounded desperate to end her life at that very moment.

Patients like her with severe depression can take drastic steps in a blink of an eye. My mind stopped working. I very well knew that if I didn't attend to her personally, she would take her life. I was the only person she trusted. On the other hand, I could imagine Kuhu's beaming face with the expectation that her Baba would cut the cake along with her. I had to choose between a life and my beloved family's expectations.

I was lost in thoughts for a minute but eventually I knew what I would choose. I chose to save the life of my mentally sick patient. I arranged an ambulance and went to her residence. She already popped a few sleeping pills but we could save her by washing her stomach quickly.

Whole night we had to struggle to stabilize the patient's condition. I returned home with a mind and body full of exhaustion, guilt. I could see Labanya sitting on the couch in our huge living hall where the celebration was arranged. Kuhu was asleep beside her, putting head on Labanya's lap. The birthday cake was still uncut on the table.

Before I could say anything, Labanya carried Kuhu in the bedroom and shut the door in front of my face. Little did I know that she also closed the door to our reconciliation along with it.

Next morning I found a note on the bedside table after waking up in the guest room. Labanya decided to leave me after enduring my ignorance towards her and Kuhu for a long time. She tagged me as an arrogant husband as well as an irresponsible father pointing out the fact that I didn't dedicate enough time to my family -which unfortunately was an undeniable fact.

My whole world went upside down. I never could think of my life without Labanya. I loved my daughter Kuhu with all my heart. But again I could not deny my irresponsibility towards them. So it was a peaceful separation without any fight. Labanya separated from me and took Kuhu along with her.

I felt a deep emptiness around me. I started spending more time in my clinic. I began to follow a strict time table throughout the day which ensures spending least time in my empty house to reduce the pain I feel every day deeply in my heart. At the end of the day, when I reach home, I still search for my lovely girl Kuhu everywhere but fail every time.

She has been staying with her mother in the USA since our separation. Every year on her birthday we talk over the phone. I believe one day Kuhu will come to see me. I am eagerly waiting for the day. Anyway, let's get back to the point. I was saying, the human mind is the most complex subject to study. It's a challenge to find out the source of mental illness and then prescribe a treatment. I have come across many strange cases of psychological problems among people.

Kamal's story stands out as one of its kind. I like to note down in my diary all the case histories that test my expertise.

It is a bright sunny day. I wake up at 6 AM, go for a jog, and after that practice some Pranayam in the park. I come back home to have shower and some breakfast. Around 10.30 AM I head towards my clinic. After reaching the clinic my receptionist Nidhi is briefing me on the list of patients and their case histories.

I take some time to go through patient's case history before meeting as it helps me to prepare. I specialise in complex mental illness which cannot be seen or realised from outside. One has to dive into the source of such abnormalities to treat them.

I see maximum are either Insomnia or anxiety patients to revisit. Only the last person in the list, Kamal is a new patient who refuses to disclose anything about his problem. He must have been suffering from insomnia like other middle-aged males and most probably something about her wife has been troubling him.

Plenty of my patients are jealous and possessive husbands who want to control their wives. If their wives refuse to follow as per husbands' wishes, the domestic environment turns negative and hence stress, tension causes their anxiety and insomnia. I presume Kamal is no different than a dominating husband whose male ego refuses to elaborate his problem to my receptionist Nidhi

(who is again a female!)

I think I have to deliver the same speech customized for all insomnia patients -'Don't take stress. Avoid excessive smoking and drinking to expect sound sleep.' And finally prescribe them with some mild sleeping pills. Anyway, to my surprise, the last case of that day has unfolded nothing like I have assumed. I have gotten tired after counselling all my patients. So I am planning on winding up with the last patient soon. I see Kamal entering my chamber with slow steps contaminated with hesitation.

Normally all insomnia patients develop dark shadows under their eyes because of sleepless nights. I try to observe Kamal closely. Kamal's face seems rather tired as if he wanted to sleep for a long time with a trace of black shadow under his eyes. He flashes a beautiful smile, an unsuccessful attempt to hide the sorrow behind it.

I greet him with a welcoming smile and point to a chair for him to take a seat. I strike the conversation first. "So Mr.Kamal, tell me how I can help you. Please don't hide anything from me. If I don't know what is exactly bothering you, I can't help you.", I speak in a soft voice yet in a professional way to gain confidence and waited for his response.

For the next 10 minutes Kamal shifts sides on the chair several times, opens mouth twice but can't say anything and in between tries to leave my chamber several times only to come back each time with the same hesitance and a shy smile on his face.

"Please calm down Kamal. Sit down on the chair and take your time. I know you didn't come to discuss your problem with me. You wouldn't hesitate so much if the problem is about you. Men, especially husbands, are very careful about disclosing any problem regarding their wives.

Love and affection towards the wife make it even tougher for the husband to disclose a single word regarding the trouble of their marital life. Your protective mind has been stopping you all along to say anything about your worry for your wife. Let me help you out. I will try to guess something about you and the reason you are here. Correct me where I am wrong." I try to encourage Kamal to express his problem without hesitation.

Finally, my words have some impact on Kamal. He looks up at me as if he can find a ray of hope. He nods as a sign of consent. I proceed with my hypothesis. "Kamal, as per the personal details provided by you in the form, I can see that you kept the part that requires information about your spouse, blank.

Your unwillingness to reveal anything about your wife has made me assume that she is quite younger to you. Maybe your wife is in the mid twenty to late twenty age group. Also your protective mindset towards her points to the fact that she is a beautiful lady. Her beauty makes you think that you have to give her extra protection. Something about your wife has been troubling you. But you are quite hesitant to be open about it."

I pause expecting some reaction from Kamal. He has been listening to me like an obedient student all along and his silence assures me that my hypothesis has been absolutely correct. "Please be open about your problem, Kamal. You can not bury all your worries inside you. If you keep your mouth shut today and go back home, your worries won't go away. Rather they will crawl back to you again and again. You need help, so ask for it. I am your best friend now who can show you a way to get rid of whatever you are facing now."

I pushed Kamal to come out of his hesitancy to share and confide in me. I have succeeded in my effort to make Kamal vocal about his worries. I brace myself only to listen to one of the most intriguing stories I have ever heard from my patients.

I pen it all down in my diary.

CHAPTER FOUR

Kamal

My good name is Kamal Banerjee. I belong to a lower middle-class family. My father was a primary school teacher in a small village ,Maynapur. I was quite good in my studies. I have had the most affectionate and supportive parents. Everything was going well in life until that inauspicious day.

When I was fifteen years old, something happened which turned my world upside down. One day I went fishing with my friends to the nearby river. I couldn't balance and fell into the water. As none of us knew swimming, I kept drowning and lost my senses.

When I opened my eyes next, I found myself covered with mud and surrounded by lots of people. All the villagers were looking at me with utter shock and fear as if they encountered some ghost! I really couldn't make out what happened to me after I drowned. It was obvious that I was rescued afterwards but I was covered by dry mud not by the wet, sticky ones of the river. I was still in a daze when my mother came running towards me and dragged me away from the crowd.

It took several days to get back to normal life. I kept asking my parents how I was saved and what happened after that. But they were surprisingly silent as if guarding some formidable secret. My regular life was not the same as before.

All my fellow mates and neighbours were acting distant and weird. They whispered to each other pointing at me .My very existence frightened them to the core. None of my friends were ready to play with me or even talk to me like they used to do before, as if they were somehow afraid of me. I had been suffering from depression.

As days passed, I became a loner, nothing but an unsocial existence. I started to keep everything to myself. My feelings, thoughts were just my own. People who knew me started to avoid me. People who didn't know me made it a point not to cross my path next time. Gradually I learnt to survive amidst hateful people.

After a few years, I completed my graduation and took a job in Kolkata. I shifted to Kolkata and started staying in a mess. Because of my aloof nature, I couldn't make any friends in this vast city. In office also I avoided any gathering as I was afraid that my social presence might scare other colleagues away. Few years later my father died and I brought my mother to Kolkata.

I rented a two-bedroom house for me and Ma. Ma wanted to marry me off as soon as possible. She was worried about me as she realised very well that after her death there would be none to look after me. I met a couple of girls for marriage purposes. But after a few meetings all of them rejected me.

They were even afraid to meet me alone after a few meetings. I could never make out the actual reason for their rejection. I have always been a decent fellow. Never ever in my life have I misbehaved or dishonoured any woman. Anyway, I accepted my bad luck and left any hope of marriage. But Ma was still hopeful. She never gave up searching for a suitable match for me.

When I was nearing my 35th birthday, I met Shikha. Shikha was Ma's friend's daughter. Her parents were also searching for a suitable groom for Shikha. We really gelled up quickly and surprisingly, she didn't leave me after a couple of meetings. So finally, I was hopeful

about our marriage. But everything changed on the day I went to their house as Shikha was not picking up my call the entire day. It was a sunny afternoon. I knocked on her door with a bunch of roses in my hand. She opened the door and was shocked to death seeing me outside as if she saw some ghost!!

She looked inside her house once and then looked at me again. She started shivering with enormous fear in her eyes. The next moment she collapsed and lost her senses. I went inside to find the reason for her breakdown but to my surprise, there was none else at her house.

So, I took her to hospital myself and informed her family. That was our last meeting. Since that event, Shikha has refused to meet or talk to me ever. I tried to meet her to ask what was my fault in all these but never got the chance. My heart sank in grief and I vowed not to get married ever!!

After a few years Ma also left me alone in this world. I got very upset and felt very lonely all the time. Anyhow days passed by. I also learnt to live a deserted sad life. I thought I would die lonely, lying on bed. There would be none beside me to hold my hand. Such negative thoughts clouded my mind all the time and made me upset. But God had something else in store for me.

Few months ago, Narayan uncle from our village along with his 18 years old granddaughter came to Kolkata to meet me. My father was very close to him. Nanda, Narayan uncle's granddaughter, is the most beautiful girl I have ever seen in my life. At first Narayan uncle told me that he came to Kolkata for a few days to finish some work. As Nanda is an orphan, she accompanied her grandfather everywhere.

Nanda appeared to be a very shy girl and used to talk less. She picked up all household chores in her hand. In her presence, I could feel homely warmth.

After a few weeks, one fine day, Narayan uncle left in a hurry for some urgent work. Whole day there was no trace of him. After waiting for two days, I got tense and was going to report to the nearby police station but Nanda stopped me. She found a letter inside Narayan uncle's trunk which was written by Narayan uncle addressing me.

In the letter, Narayan uncle confessed his wish of Nanda's marriage to me. He was incapable of looking after her anymore. His sudden visit, leaving Nanda behind-all were pre-planned. When I told Nanda whatever was written in the letter, she smiled. I realised that Nanda knew all of it beforehand. I couldn't believe that a beautiful, young girl like Nanda would accept a much older guy like me as her husband. I asked her if she was ready for this marriage. To my endless joy , she said, "yes!"

We got married soon. My new life with Nanda started with a happy note. Like a responsible wife she was taking good care of me . She made my tiny house a home. Definitely we were a mismatch for an ideal couple but we were satisfied with our own lives. After a busy office day when I returned home , Nanda's warm greetings used to take away all my tiredness. Nanda laughed at my silly jokes, and I praised her cooking skill. Friday was our "Movie Night". We used to enjoy movies together at home.Life was calm,composed, satisfying.

But little did I know that my bad luck was still chasing me. My happy married life didn't last for long. One night

I found Nanda in the washroom , all wet and talking gibberish. When I tried to talk to her she reacted as if she saw some ghost, as if she even didn't know me! She had been senseless for a few hours . When she woke up ,she didn't say a single word. I tried to comfort her but she shut me down and looked at me with utter disgust and fear. She vigorously kept denying that I am his husband.

She mentioned myself as 'the other one'. No matter how many times I tried to prove herself wrong, she was rigid at her place. That night an unrecoverable distance was created between us. ' Trust'- the base of our relationship broke down.

Nanda is now refusing to stay with me anymore . But she has nowhere to go also . All day long she locks herself in a room. She lets herself out only when I am not at home. I have lost all my hope and my patience. I don't know how to help her if she is not ready to talk to me. Few days ago, my office colleague gave me your reference.

At first I was unsure and apprehensive to reveal my personal married life to some unknown person but later I thought Nanda might open up to someone else if not to me. Still it took many sleepless nights and enormous courage to make a decision to visit here. My earnest request to you- please help us. I don't know where else to go if you don't help me. Nanda won't agree to come here with me as she doesn't trust me anymore.

But she is friendly in nature. She likes to host guests a lot, especially if the guest is an aged person like you. She lost her mother and her father never took her responsibility. A father figure like you may soften her heart enough to be open about all her fears and worries.

So you can come to my house as my distant relative and talk to her. I know that I am requesting you to do something absurd. But I can't see any other way to make Nanda meet you. Please come to my house once. I am begging you!

****

Kamal breaks down in front of Dr.Ranjan . He can not stop tears rolling down his cheeks. But he feels better after revealing all his hidden emotions, feelings which have been killing him from inside for a long time. After meeting the doctor, he can again see a ray of hope.

'If he can arrange the meeting between Doctor and Nanda, definitely Nanda would be able to recover from her sickness and they can again lead a happy life together.' Kamal's hopeful mind keeps telling this to him.

CHAPTER FIVE

Dr.Ranjan

I feel really sorry for Kamal after listening to his story. I see a hopeless person tired from fighting his bad luck continuously. He found happiness very late in his life and he is not ready to let it go at any cost. He looks up to me as the last key to restore happiness in his life.

Being a doctor, I always encourage patients to come for consultation in my chamber. It's very important that Nanda realises that there's something wrong with her mental health and she needs help. Self- realisation is the first step towards her treatment.

But from Kamal's story I can make out that Nanda is not in the position realise the gravity of her condition. She is drowned into a world of hallucinations where her mind makes up two versions of her husband Kamal. There is a possibility that she had to marry Kamal as she had nowhere to go or Kamal might force her to marry being thrilled with her beauty.

There are many more possibilities which can lead her mind to such hallucinations. Treatment can be done if the cause of disease is revealed. So I have to talk to Nanda to find out what has been troubling her.

Some elements in Kamal's case are very interesting and different from other cases I have treated in my life. My curiosity made me pay a visit to Kamal's house the next afternoon to meet Nanda. It is decided that Kamal will inform Nanda that his uncle(that's me) will come for lunch at his house. It's evident that Nanda will not feel free to say anything at Kamal's presence. So we plan that, after lunch Kamal will make some excuse and go out for some time. Meanwhile I will try to strike a friendly discussion with Nanda.

Next afternoon I reach Kamal's address. It is a four storied building at the southern east part of the city. Kamal stays in a small one bedroom flat on the second floor. I find Kamal at the door waiting for me. He welcomes me heartily to his living room. We sit on the sofa. He seems quite happy seeing me and becomes busy to accommodate me with all the comforts. He announces my arrival to Nanda . He has been talking to me continuously and laughing at silly jokes for last few minuites to confirm our familiarity.

After a while a beautiful young lady enters the drawing room. Kamal introduces Nanda as his wife. Once Kamal has told me that he has never seen any girl as beautiful as Nanda and I can't agree less after meeting her. She has a porcelain like complexion with perfect features. She could have been married to a far better person than Kamal in every aspect, I admit to myself.

Kamal is definitely lucky to have a wife as gorgeous as Nanda. Her youthful face reminds me of Kuhu, my beloved daughter. Nanda greets me with 'pranam' and I bless her from the core of my heart. I feel sad thinking about Nanda's mental illness.

Nanda sits in a chair far from Kamal. I am trying to strike a conversation but Nanda doesn't seem comfortable talking much in front of Kamal. At lunch I find out that Nanda is not only a good looking young lady but also an excellent cook! Nanda beams with happiness when I appreciate her cooking ability. In fact this is the first time I see her smiling. To encourage her we keep discussing some famous recipes and that helps Nanda to be more expressive. After lunch Kamal goes out to bring some sweet dishes. Nanda somehow looks relieved as Kamal leaves. She seems to be more comfortable being with a stranger like me than she is with her husband, Kamal. I prepare myself to utilise the alone time to know more about Nanda.

I start asking simple questions to her. Her nervousness is quite evident. She is taking time, preparing herself to share the darkest secret in her life. At first she needs to trust me completely. It's not easy to display our inner insecurity, fear, doubts which we deny to ourselves also. But now Nanda has to let go and confront her fear. I am waiting for her.

Nanda is visibly apprehensive to respond while I ask her about childhood. She has tried to avoid my questions several times. I can confidently conclude about her terrible experience in childhood. I guess I have to convince her to be more comfortable and open about her past.

I have not revealed my real identity, actual reason of my visit. I feel an urge to speak the truth as it will not be fair to keep an innocent girl like Nanda in darkness. Maybe the reality can make her realise the gravity of the problem and encourage her to share her feelings and emotions to me, to a doctor who can help her.

I have only heard Kamal's side of story. Now I want to know what Nanda has to say about the conflict between her and Kamal. What has made her so fearful of her own husband? I brief everything to Nanda from Kamal's visit at my chamber to our today's meeting at their house. After few minutes of silence, she starts speaking slowly but confidently.

CHAPTER SIX

Nanda

My name is Nanda Chatterjee. I belong to an orthodox Brahmin family. My father married my non-Brahmin mother without grandfather's consent. My grandfather Narayan Chatterjee was a 'Pandit' in Sanskrit. He used to teach Sanskrit in the village school. He was very strict in matters of caste and creed. He disowned my father for marrying my mother and made it clear there was no place for him in his house. My father was a homeopath doctor. He settled down in a nearby town with my mother. They were happy together.

After two years of marriage my mother got pregnant with me. I was an unlucky girl to lose my mother at birth. My father broke down after mother's death. He wasn't able to take care of me and left me at my grandfather's place.

As I was carrying Brahmin blood, I was welcomed heartily there. I grew up under the shelter of my grandparents. I started going to school and it was all fine until something strange happened. I was at nineth standard and our final examination was going on.

I was busy writing my paper. Suddenly I saw Amaresh standing at the door. Amaresh was my childhood friend, our neighbour Nibaran kaka's son. Amaresh left our village two years ago to stay with his maternal uncle. I was surprised to see him here after so long. Before I could call him, he left.

After my examination I went to Amaresh's house to meet him but Nibaran uncle Amaresh`s father, told that Amaresh was still at his uncle's house. He never came back to Village since he left! I was quite shocked as I was pretty sure that I saw Amaresh in broad daylight at my school! Anyway, preparation for the examination didn't leave me much time to think over what happened.

Few days passed after that event. My examination was over and it was a quiet afternoon. I was reading a book lying on my bed. Suddenly I could hear someone calling my name. I turned my head away from the book and looked around. I saw Amaresh standing outside the window, smiling at me.

"Uff Amaresh, you startled me! When did you come and why were you standing outside?" I welcomed him inside but found him standing there only ignoring several requests.

I was freaking at his creepy smile. Something was not feeling right. I gathered all my courage and stepped out of the room but found none outside! How could one vanish in such a small time frame!! I couldn't take the shock and lost my senses.

After that event I started seeing Amaresh from time to time at different places but each time I was assured that in reality he never returned to our village. I had never had any romantic feeling towards Amaresh that would make me hallucinate so much. The hallucination seemed so real that it started scaring me.

So to break my doubt, I decided to talk to Amaresh on the phone. I collected his uncle's landline number and called. Amaresh answered the call and was very delighted hearing my voice. We talked about our studies, old childhood days and many other things. Lastly, I asked him if he visited our village recently. His answer was negative. I felt relieved knowing the fact from Amaresh himself. I was sure that I imagined everything. I was about to hang up the call and the very moment I saw Amaresh standing under a banyan tree smiling at me! The other Amaresh was still talking on the phone.

I closed my eyes and hoped to see none under the banyan tree once I opened them. But a chill passed down my spine while I saw Amaresh still standing under the tree. Amaresh on the phone kept talking but I couldn't concentrate on any of his words. I hung up the call to leave immediately.

As soon as I stepped out of the telephone booth, the other Amaresh started coming towards me fast. I panicked and ran towards home from there.

Upon reaching home I lost my senses and woke up the next day with high fever. It took one month for my full recovery and I became very weak. I joined my school and tried to get back to my normal life. I thought after that call I would stop seeing Amaresh. But to my dismay, I started spotting Amaresh again. Strangely, Amaresh had been getting healthier and stronger each time I saw him. Though my hallucinations were still there, I had been trying to ignore them.

Few months later I got a call from Amaresh. He sounded very weak on the phone. He informed me that since the day we talked last, his health had been deteriorating. He became so weak that he couldn't eat, walk or do anything by himself. I was shocked because the Amaresh I had been seeing from time to time was quite healthy.

My grandfather showed me to village doctors but none could find out the real reason of my physical weakness or mental instability. Sometimes I would scream even at the presence of my friends or grandparents whom I had known since childhood. My condition had been deteriorating fast. Finally, I was taken to a city doctor who prescribed me some medicine and advised therapy sessions regularly. In few weeks I started feeling better. My terrible hallucinations had been disappearing slowly. I started behaving normally. Most importantly I stopped seeing that other Amaresh time to time.

Few months later I got a call from Amaresh. He sounded very weak on the phone. He informed me that since the day we talked last, his health had been deteriorating. He became so weak that he couldn't eat, walk or do anything by himself. I was shocked because the Amaresh I had been seeing from time to time was quite healthy.

I couldn't find any answer to this mystery. But I was worried for my friend "Amaresh" as I got a feeling that something bad was happening to him and somehow the other Amaresh was responsible for that. I couldn't share my thoughts to anyone as none would have believed me.

Few weeks later Nibaran uncle came to our house with some sweets. He informed us that Amaresh came to see him last night after a long time. He was very happy as Amaresh scored well in his examination. I was also happy thinking that Amaresh must have regained his good health. Nothing bad happened to him. I decided to pay a visit to Nibaran uncle's house and meet Amaresh.

Next day after noon I was finishing my homework in my room. Suddenly I could hear my grandfather calling my name from the living room. I saw Amaresh chatting with my grandfather once I entered the room. He looked healthy and as smiling as always. After a while grandfather left us alone and went out for some work. The moment I was alone with Amaresh, I started feeling awkward. It wasn't that I was feeling shy or there were any romantic vibes between us. The way he was talking felt quite different from the way he used to talk on the phone.

Still that was not enough to raise any doubt. When I picked up a topic about which we spoke over phone, he seemed uncomfortable and denied that he ever spoke to me on phone at all!! Moreover he complained that he came to meet me often but I ignored him!

I still remember that he said, "Oh Nandu! So many times I came to see you, to talk to you but you pretended as if you couldn't see me! I really fell in love with you Nandu. The day I saw you for the first time, I knew you were the one I had been looking for. Forget your childhood friend Amaresh. He is a weak, shy and unsmart fellow. Absolutely a mismatch for a beautiful, young girl like you! This Amaresh is strong, expressive and powerful. We will have a wonderful life together. Don't think so much! I have come to take you with me."

I realised that the person sitting in front of me was an imposter. He was not my childhood friend. I never talked to him on the phone. He came from darkness. I could smell lust and greed in his words. Many questions were popping up in my mind like- 'What happened to the real Amaresh? Where was he? Did that imposter harm him?'

Suddenly his wicked smile passed the chill down my spine. "Don't think too much about that poor, weak Amaresh. He is gone. I have replaced him. Come with me Nandu. We will be happy together."- He said.

I screamed in fear and lost my senses. When I woke up, I saw my grandmother's scared face leaning upon me.

I checked again and again if that imposter was there. Grandmother told me I had been senseless for a few hours. When they found me lying on the floor, they could not see Amaresh there. I felt quite relieved but scared to think about what happened earlier. One week after this event Amaresh died at his uncle's house. They brought his body to the village house for cremation. I was shocked to see his skeletal body. Yes, his body looked as if all energy, nutrition had been sucked out for long. Nibaran uncle was speechless. None could think of a reason behind his death.

Amaresh's death affected me mentally. I couldn't go out anywhere alone out of fear. I locked myself inside my room. I couldn't eat or sleep properly. Always I felt a presence around me. My grandparents showed me to the doctor. After a few months of treatment, I recovered.

I completed my higher secondary and then graduation. Unfortunately, my grandmother died in a couple of months of my graduation. My grandfather broke down completely and decided to marry me off as soon as possible. He found out about Mr. Kamal Banerjee from a distant relative.

He planned to visit his place and arrange our marriage. We came to his house. He seemed like a very polite and helpful person. My grandfather was supposed to approach him with a marriage proposal. But one day he left the house leaving a letter for Mr.Kamal and never came back.

I knew that in the letter grandfather requested for marriage. I guessed that my grandfather didn't have enough money to sponsor my marriage. Hence the disappearance act. Still Mr.Kamal waited quite a few days for my grandfather but he never returned.

We married in a registry office in a simple manner. I knew my husband was much older than me but I liked the kind of person he was. Our married life was peaceful. My husband is a soft-spoken person with no high ambition. We had been living an uneventful, simple routine life and I liked it that way.

He was very affectionate and caring towards me. Everything was fine until one night 'the other one' appeared. That imposter looked exactly like my husband but his lusty eyes, wicked smile told me he was not Kamal. 'The other one' tried to touch me. I could barely escape and locked myself inside the washroom.

Whole night he kept knocking on the door. I was shaking in fear. I fell asleep after some time. When I opened my eyes, I saw our neighbourhood aunty and my husband. There was no trace of that imposter. I felt relieved. I tried to explain everything that happened that night but none of them believed me. They thought it was just a bad dream, nothing else. I also tried to calm myself down.

I could notice changes in my husband since that night. He became more talkative and also aggressive. His attitude changed totally. He became loud and possessive. He stopped going to the office to keep an eye on me. He doubted that I might have an extra marital affair.

I realised that the imposter possessed my husband. I could feel the same lust, greed and darkness I felt about that imposter Amaresh. I keep myself locked in a room to protect myself from that demon at day time. In the evening the demon leaves my husband and he becomes gentle, soft spoken. The same old Kamal.

I tried to make him understand about 'the other one' but he never tried to believe me. He has been becoming thinner and weaker day by day. I am scared because the same thing happened to Amaresh before his death.

Ranjan uncle, maybe I am a village girl but I am educated enough to guess that you are invited here not for just lunch. My husband doubts that I have been suffering from mental illness like hallucinations. I know you are the doctor whom he consulted for my treatment.

Kamal thinks that the problem lies within me but the truth is he needs help. I have told you everything you need to know. Please start treatment for Kamal. Chase that other one away from our lives. Otherwise, he will ruin Kamal. I will lose my husband forever.

I have nowhere to go from here. This is my only shelter. Please help us!

Nanda started crying helplessly. She seems scared to stay with Kamal as if he is possessed (!). At the same time, she can not leave him out of her love and respect for husband. Dr. Ranjan feels bad for Nanda. He assures her that he will try his best to help them.

CHAPTER SEVEN

Dr.Ranjan

I could not sleep for several nights thinking about this strange case of Nanda and Kamal. Kamal is sure that Nanda have been hallucinating and needs proper treatment. Surely the idea of 'the other one' or 'demonic possession' seems absurd. Nanda has suffered from some trauma in her childhood.

She has lost her mother at birth. She has been deprived from father's affection whole life. Her traumatic mind may have given birth to 'the other one'. She has been very much afraid of this trauma. She can't face it and lost senses whenever 'the other one' appears. But I need more information to reach a more constructive conclusion about Nanda's condition.

On the other hand, I observed some distinct changes in Kamal's behaviour. He was very soft spoken, confused the day he visited my chamber. But at his home he was talkative and confident. Even, his tone and walking style were different from the other day. Most strikingly, in the chamber he used his right hand to pick up his handkerchief from the ground while at home he took his glass up with left hand!

May be Kamal is a patient of schizophrenia. Maybe he has displayed different personalities from time to time and hence Nanda has discovered 'the other one'. Again, in Kamal's case I need more information to build a foundation for my theory. I have decided to visit Maynapur, Kamal's native place. I am certain to gather some helpful inputs regarding this case.

CHAPTER EIGHT

Maynapur

The hired jeep rattles along the dirt road, raising plumes of dust in its wake. Dr.Ranjan squints through the windshield at the small village ahead - Maynapur, according to the faded sign. The birthplace of Kamal, his newest patient, the reason he has made this journey to the middle of nowhere.

As the jeep approaches the village, children playing in the street scatters like startled birds. A few curious faces peers from doorways and windows, but most of the huts nearby remains still and silent. An ominous quiet blanketed the dusty streets.

Dr.Ranjan pulls up outside the village chai shop, killing the engine. He brushes dust from his shirt and slicks back his greying hair as he climbs down from the jeep, plastering on his most welcoming smile.

"Namaste!" he calls out in a hearty voice as he approaches an old man seated on a wooden stool, puffing away on a bidi. "I'm Dr.Ranjan from Calcutta. I was hoping someone could help me locate the Banerjee family home?"

The old man stares at him impassively, then spits a thick stream of betel juice onto the ground between them in reply. Dr. Ranjan's smile freezes on his face as he takes an involuntary step backwards.

He turns and knocks on the door of the ramshackle hut beside the chai stall, peering through the dingy window. A haggard woman's face appears briefly before the curtains snap shut again. He knocks louder, calling out in his friendliest tone, but the only response is a muffled shout in a local dialect he can't comprehend.

Over the next hour, Dr. Ranjan has made his way through the village only experiencing the hostility and fear radiating from every soot-stained window and slammed door. He has failed to garner more than a few wary glances and hushed whispers.

Finally, sweating and flustered, Dr. Ranjan has found himself back at the jeep empty-handed. The old man has vanished from the chai stall, leaving only a few stray chickens scratching in the dust.

"What horrors lie in this place?" Dr. Ranjan murmurs. "And what happened to you here, Kamal?"

The sun begins to dip behind the trees, painting the sky in streaks of blood orange. Dr. Ranjan feels a cold shiver trickle down his spine. This village is hiding something...and he fears he may never uncover what secrets have been buried amidst Maynapur's cracked walls and shuttered homes. Dr. Ranjan prepares to give up his search for the day. Just then, a stooped figure emerges from one of the huts.

"Saheb?" a reedy voice called out. "Are you looking for someone?"

Dr. Ranjan spins around. "Yes, yes! I'm Dr. Ranjan from Calcutta. I'm trying to locate the family of a patient of mine - Kamal Banerjee. Can you help me?"

The old man's face remains impassive, giving nothing away. "I knew of the Banerjee family once. But they are gone now." Dr.Ranjan presses. "What can you tell me about

Kamal Banerjee?"

The old man shakes his head slowly. "Some things are better left buried, Saheb. Forget Kamal Banerjee. Nothing good will come of digging up the past."

As he turns to shuffle away, Dr. Ranjan steps forward urgently. "Wait! Please...I mean no trouble, but I must know what happened with Kamal. How long have you known him? I want to know everything about him."

"Very well, Saheb. But you may not believe whatever I am going to say." He glances around the deserted street with what seems like fear. "Not here. Come with me."

The old man leads the way toward his hut, casting furtive looks over his shoulder. As the tin door creaks open, Dr. Ranjan settles cross-legged on the dirt floor. The old man accepts the bidi Dr. Ranjan offers in thanks.

"My name is Nidhiram Saha," he says at last in a whisper.

.

CHAPTER NINE

Nidhiram

I was a primary school teacher in this village. I had known Kamal since his birth. His father was my colleague. Kamal was a studious and obedient boy. His father was very proud of Kamal. When Kamal was about Fifteen years old, he went fishing with his friends. Accidentally he slipped and fell into the water. He drowned in the water as he didn't know how to swim.

We had to drag his body out of water. He was dead, there was no heartbeat or breathing. All of us mourned the untimely death of such a young, promising boy. As Kamal had an untimely death, his parents decided to bury his body instead of cremation.

After the burial, in the afternoon Kamal's mother was sleeping in her room. Suddenly she could hear Kamal calling her. At first, she thought she was imagining it. But she saw Kamal standing on their premises and calling her name. Kamal's body was covered with mud. Kamal's mother screamed with shock. We all rushed there and our conditions were no different than Kamal's mother.

We couldn't believe our eyes. We buried his dead body in our own hands!! Human beings can't defy death, only a demon can. We were sure that the devil must have possessed Kamal's dead body and returned with some evil purpose. None went near him.

We called a village exorcist to save Kamal from devil's possession. The exorcist came but didn't succeed in his task. That devil was so strong that he chased the exorcist away. We villagers fled from the place out of fear. Kamal lost his senses immediately. His parents took him inside. After a few days Kamal could be seen here and there in the village just like a normal human being. We started to believe the whole event as the almighty's miracle rather than demonic possession.

Few months passed by. We almost accepted Kamal's past but some unusual events came into the picture. People started to experience Kamal in two different personalities. Sometimes Kamal behaved like the same old 'soft spoken, gentle' Kamal. But sometimes he used to become very aggressive and loud.

He started arguing and fighting with his friends and family. Surprisingly he couldn't remember anything of that at the next moment. His behaviour intrigued fear among us. A strong belief got instilled in our minds that the devil never left Kamal. Hence Kamal had been behaving so strangely.

It may be unexpected that being a school teacher myself, how could I believe in such superstition. But what I saw in my eyes, how can I deny that! It was a moonlit night. I was returning from a student's house after taking tuitions. Though it was 10 at night, everything was visible in the moonlight. I was crossing the road that passed through the forest area as it was a shortcut to my house.

Suddenly I stopped hearing some sound. I didn't expect anyone at that time in the forest. People were scared to use the forest road as they believed the forest was haunted and some evil spirit could be seen at night.

I inspected everywhere around me but couldn't see anyone. I started walking fast towards my home. Suddenly I could hear someone calling me- ' Sir, Nidhiram Sir, please stop. Please take me with you. Don't leave me.' Again, I stopped to find out the owner of that voice. I thought one of my students was in danger. He might have gotten lost in the forest and needed help. But I found none nearby.

For one moment I thought I might be imagining everything. Suddenly a coconut fell down in front of me. I looked up and to my utter shock, I saw Kamal at the top of the coconut tree. He started laughing out loud and said, "Nidhiram Sir, do you want a coconut? Coconut water is good for your health."

I knew that it could not be Kamal. At 5 years of age, Kamal fell down from a banyan tree. Since then he had been afraid of heights and he had never climbed any tree. If he wasn't Kamal, then who or what was that!! Unknown fear sieged me and I fled away from that spot. I still could hear his wicked smile.

Next day I went to Kamal's house to ask about last night. Kamal's mother said that Kamal had been suffering from fever for a few days and didn't leave the house last night. My doubt became stronger. Whom I saw that night was not Kamal. Like me many people saw this other Kamal in different places in awkward, scary situations.

We tried to avoid Kamal out of fear. After that many years passed. Kamal finished school and went to the city for graduation. After his father's death, he took his mother with him. It had been fifteen years. He never returned to this village. The villagers have been always afraid of Kamal. None takes his name or discusses about him since his departure. As you have come to our village after all these years to enquire about him, I am sure the devil must have possessed him again!!

****

Nidhiram refuses to say anything more about Kamal after repeated requests from Dr.Ranjan. So Dr. Ranjan decides to visit another part of the village where Nanda used to stay with her grandparents. Dr. Ranjan hurries back to his jeep, Nidhiram's horrific story has been replaying endlessly in his mind. He knows he is totally unwelcome in this village. He may be chased away if he asks anymore questions to anyone but something compels him to stay - the haunted look in Kamal's eyes, the questions that still burn.

Locating Kamal's wife Nanda in this village proves no easier a task. He can hear muttered curses drifted from doorways as he asks about Nanda: "...the devil's spawn...unnatural...eats the flesh of men..."

Clearly, whatever obscure fears have gripped the villagers go beyond the Banerjee family's tragedy - they seem to view Nanda herself as some sort of demonic presence.

Still, he persists in his inquiries with grim determination, refusing to be cowed by suspicious glares and outright hostility. After much efforts, finally he is able to track down a betel-stained old man willing to point him towards Nanda's maternal uncle's hut.

"Motilal keeps to himself these days," the toothless local cackles. "After whatever his devil niece has done, can't say I blame him..."

The rickety hut sits isolated at the edge of the village, surrounded by a crumbling stone fence. Dr.Ranjan's hammering on the weathered door goes unanswered for so long, he begins to fear the place abandoned. Just as he prepares to give up, a gravelly voice rings out from within.

"State your business and be gone with you! I want no trouble from outsiders..."

Ranjan clears his throat. "Sir, I mean no harm! My name is Dr. Ranjan, and I've come seeking information about your niece Nanda - the wife of my patient, Kamal Banerjee. It's a matter of life and death, I'm afraid."

A protracted silence follows, stretching out interminably. Then a narrow slit appears in the doorway. A single bloodshot eye regard Dr. Ranjan warily.

"Your patient's name is Kamal Banerjee, you say? That devil's brood is Nandu`s husband?"

Dr. Ranjan fights to keep his tone respectful. "I understand there are stories about what happened here. But Nanda is gravely ill, perhaps dying. For her sake, and Kamal's, I beg you to tell me what you know."

Another endless pause, the door flows open. Stale smoke overwhelms him as he goes inside. The heavy door slams shut behind him.Blinking in the gloom, Dr. Ranjan finds himself face-to-face with Motilal. The old man's sunken features and matted beard gives him the appearance of a walking corpse.

"You truly know nothing, do you, daktaar-sheb?" Motilal's foul breath washes over Ranjan's face. "About the darkness that lives within that wretched girl...and the unholy appetites she birthed in this village long ago?"

"You wish to hear my poor Nandu's story?" he rasped. "Then hear it you shall, daktaar-sheb...and pray the images I plant in your brain do not breed nightmares to torment you forever more..."

CHAPTER TEN

Motilal

My name is Motilal Kundu. Nanda's mother Bindu was my cousin. She was like my own sister. We had been brought up in the same neighbourhood. Our families were quite close. We went to the same school. We played together, in fact we were best friends. We completed our school together. After school my parents sent me to town to finish my graduation.

Bindu was an exceptionally good looking girl. She was quiet, introvert and hardly spoke to any outsider. We were quite surprised when we come to know she had been having an affair with a Brahmin boy, named Rakesh. We never thought that Bindu could have an affair, moreover with a Brahmin boy. Rakesh's father Narayan Chatterjee was dead against this relationship. But Rakesh was deeply in love with Bindu. They fled from the village together and got married in the town.

Rakesh started his homeopathy practice there and started a new life with Bindu. After a few years of marriage, Bindu got pregnant with Nanda. She came back to the village during her pregnancy as there was none to take care of her in the town. Rakesh had been busy with his practice the whole day.

At that time, I came back to the village after completing my graduation. I used to spend my time with Bindu to keep her cheerful. After a few months of pregnancy, Bindu started behaving weird. She used to blabber nonsense. Sometimes she cried continuously. I tried to calm her down but she couldn't stand me either.

At first, I overlooked her behaviour thinking of 'pregnancy mood swings'. Later her activities aggravated to the extreme. She strongly believed that the baby in her womb was the devil's daughter. She used to say, "This is not a normal baby growing inside my womb. She is a Pishachini (Devil's daughter). She has been eating me from inside. She will not let me live as I know her secret. She will eat you all! She has great hypnotic power. You all will be under her spell. She won't spare anyone!!"

Her condition was getting worse day by day. She became so thin that one could count her bones. She wanted to kill her own baby by starving. But surprisingly her womb was growing while Bindu was thinning. We consulted a doctor for her degrading condition. Doctor prescribed sleeping pills and nutritious food for her.

But we couldn't convince Bindu to take proper food and medicine. She became more violent thinking that we were trying to poison her. We had to watch her health worsening helplessly. Under such situations, one night her labour pain induced and she could not bear the pain and lost her senses. We took her to a nearby hospital. After a whole night's struggle, she gave birth to Nanda. Her body was too weak to bear the delivery procedure. She breathed her last after giving birth to Nanda.

Nanda was a beautiful healthy baby. Rakesh was very upset at Bindu's untimely demise. He couldn't welcome Nanda heartily. Like other people he also held Nanda responsible for Bindu's death. Rakesh left for town leaving Nanda with her grandparents. Narayan Chatterjee used to love his granddaughter very much. He and his wife were bringing up Nanda with all their love and care. I grew so fond of Nanda that I settled in the village only. I took a job in primary school as a teacher. Every day I used to take Nanda to school and in the evening I taught her at home. As days passed, Nanda grew into a lovely young lady. She was doing quite well in studies also. Everything was going well until that unpleasant event happened.

Amaresh was Nanda's childhood friend. They grew up together. After a few years of school, Amaresh was caught smoking ganja in the classroom. The school authorities expelled him. His parents sent him to town at his uncle's place. One day after school, Nanda said that she saw Amaresh at her school but before she could say anything he left.

I thought that Amaresh might come back to the village. Nanda went to see Amaresh at his place though I was not comfortable with Nanda mixing with spoilt boys like Amaresh. Later we came to know that Nanda couldn't meet Amaresh as he never returned to the village. So I convinced Nanda that it was her imagination.

Since that event Nanda used to remain disturbed. Often she asked if Amaresh came to the village. She even tried to talk to him over the phone. She was getting obsessed with Amaresh. She was having hallucinations. Most of the time she remained at home. In school also friends started avoiding her because of weird behaviour. She kept saying, "I can see the demon everywhere. He looks like Amaresh. But I know it's not him. The demon will kill Amaresh."

After a few months, Amaresh came to the village. He paid a visit to Nanda. Nanda fell sick once Amaresh left. We had no Idea of what happened between them. Few weeks later Amaresh died of malnutrition. The news was shocking to us because last time when we saw Amaresh he seemed quite healthy.

Local people along with Amaresh's family started blaming Nanda for his death. She was again tagged as 'Pishachini' who sucked out all life power from Amaresh. People started cursing her and made her life miserable. Nanda stopped stepping outside her house. She went under severe depression. She also thought herself responsible for whatever happened to Amaresh. Thankfully she continued her studies and completed graduation sitting at private examination.

Her grandfather had been trying to marry her off. Though Nanda was an extremely beautiful and educated girl, none was ready to accept her as a bride because of her past history. Still people were quite convinced that she had demonic power and would kill everyone to quench her blood thirst. Meanwhile Nanda's grandmother fell sick due to mental stress. She loved Nanda very dearly. She brought up Nanda with motherly affection. Such ill fate of Nanda was unacceptable for her. She breathed her last after Nanda's graduation.

Both Nanda and her grandfather were overwhelmed with shock. Narayan uncle wanted to go on pilgrimage after marrying Nanda to some suitable boy. He knew very well that Nanda had to be married to some outsider. So one fine day he left the village with Nanda and never returned. I have been really worried for this poor girl. She is very dear to me. After so many days you brought her news.

****

Dr. Ranjan bids farewell to Motilal Kundu and promises to take him to Nanda soon. He has gathered important information about Kamal and Nanda. Patients' background check is very crucial in the matter of their treatment.

One coherent thread has emerged - for whatever reason, the key to unraveling Nanda's psychological turmoil appears to lie with Kamal's past romance with another woman named Shikha. He decides to meet Shikha, Kamal's ex-fiancee. Kamal and her marriage was almost decided. Suddenly what changed her mind? Dr. Ranjan is determined to find out the reason to gain more clarity about Kamal.

He returns to the city and meets with Kamal. Kamal seems quite tense as Nanda's condition have been worsening day by day. Dr. Ranjan takes details about Shikha and assures Kamal that Nanda's treatment will begin soon.

The very next day Dr. Ranjan reaches Shikha's house. Shikha's father informs him that Shikha got married a couple of years ago. She has been living with her husband in different places. Recently they have shifted to Kolkata. After what feels like an eternity of cajoling, her father has finally divulged her present address in southern Kolkata.

After inquiring a few people, Dr. Ranjan spots the humble dwelling matching the address directions in the south East part of Kolkata. He takes a steadying breath, preparing himself - who knows what secrets await with this mysterious Shikha?

The door creaks open at his knock, framing a young woman swathed in a dingy sari. Though her features are delicate, there are dark circles beneath her eyes and a wary hunch to her shoulders, as if bearing a great weariness.

"Yes? What is your business here?" Her voice is little more than a dry whisper.

Dr. Ranjan clears his throat. "Forgive me for calling so late. I'm Dr. Ranjan - I've come to discuss a...mutual acquaintance. Kamal Banerjee."

The reaction is as visceral as it is unexpected. Shikha's eyes blow wide, her face draining of colour until she clutches at the door frame for support.

"No...no, not him. I cannot..." Her words dissolves into anguished murmuring, like a prayer on a loop. "Oh merciful goddess, why now after so long?"

Alarmed, Dr. Ranjan steps forward, raising placating hands. "Please, please calm yourself! I'm here on a matter regarding Kamal's wife, Nanda..."

At the name, Shikha's head snaps up, her eyes refocusing on Ranjan with a sudden, brittle intensity. "Nanda?" She clutches her hands together tightly. "What of her? Has...has that monster done something to harm her?"

Dr. Ranjan wets his lips. This Shikha has been Kamal's lover before Nanda - and to judge by her reaction, whatever has transpired clearly still haunts her.

"I'm afraid Nanda is...unwell, mentally," he says carefully. "Traumatized in ways even she cannot explain. As her husband's doctor, I'm trying to understand what could have caused such anguish."

He holds Shikha's gaze beseechingly. "I know this is difficult, but if you know anything about Kamal's past with Nanda, I must ask you to tell me. For her sake."

Shikha stares at him for a long moment, indecision warring on her features. Then, seeming to reach some resolve, she gives a curt nod and steps back to allow him entry.

"Come in, Dr. Ranjan. And pray this knowledge does not unhinge your own sanity as it has mine..."

"Kamal and I were to be married, once upon a time," she begins in a toneless monotone. "From respected Brahmin families, it was an auspicious match blessed by both clans..."

A tremor enters her voice, fracturing it. "Until...until I saw the darkness within him. The insatiable, unholy cravings no person should ever indulge."

Dr. Ranjan feels an icy trickle trail his spine but remains silent, sensing there is more to come. Shikha pulls her shawl tighter as if warding off a chill. Dr. Ranjan can only gape in stunned silence, his mind is overloaded and reeling. He is embracing himself to hear Shikha`s story.

CHAPTER ELEVEN

Shikha

I had a chance to get to know Kamal for a couple of months. His mother was my mother's childhood friend. Our mothers wanted to marry us off. At first when I met Kamal, I really liked his humble attitude. He was simple and soft spoken. He was not like most of the men for whom lust comes in mind while being with a lady. We could feel a very good chemistry between us.

I was thinking of finalizing our marriage. I decided to meet Kamal to discuss our future plans. We were having dinner in a restaurant. Kamal seemed quite restless that day. There was a distinct change in his looks. His tone was also different. He suggested to me the idea of living together. I was shocked as Kamal appeared to be very orthodox and traditional in matters of relationship. He never even touched my hand and suddenly he wanted to stay with me under one roof without being married!

For the first time I saw lust and greed in his eyes. We had an argument that night. Kamal became aggressive and arrogant. I left without having dinner. I couldn't sleep the whole night thinking about the drastic change I observed in Kamal. Next few days I avoided meeting him as I was upset.

One day he came to my house to meet me and to my surprise he behaved as if nothing happened at dinner the other night! He was talking to me as he used to talk before. When I asked him about his idea of living together, he was shocked and requested me not to think of such a dirty concept!! I thought he must be ashamed of his behaviour. So he just didn't want to think or talk about what happened.

I decided to ignore the whole event and moved forward. Next day in the afternoon Kamal came to our house without any prior notice. I was shocked as Kamal never did anything unplanned. He was a very organised person. I was alone at home. It was an awkward situation for me but Kamal seemed very comfortable.

He started complaining about my lack of feelings and commitment towards him. He aggressively demanded for us to live together. I reminded him about the last meeting when he pretended to be dead against this ' live together' concept.

He laughed at me and said, "That must be your lousy, idiot Kamal. Can't you spot differences between him and me? I am brave and aggressive. I am a real man. You want me Shikha, not him. Accept it and come with me. We will live our lives together. "

The person in front of me was not the Kamal I knew. His lusty eyes and wicked smile made him someone else but Kamal. I lost my mind and told him to leave immediately. But Kamal forced himself on me. When I shouted out for help, he fled like a coward.

This event shattered me inside out. I no longer could accept Kamal as my life partner. I couldn't recognise Kamal's real personality at all. How could I spend my whole life with such a person!? I stopped meeting him or taking his phone calls since then. That's all I could say about Kamal.

Kamal's marital life is bound to be problematic as he behaves weird from time to time. For the first few days of meeting, it may not become evident but in time his true self is bound to come forward. He will show his ugly face in broad daylight. I strongly believe that the problem lies with Kamal not with his wife. That poor girl must have gone through hell! Please help her Dr.Ranjan. Kamal needs to be treated immediately or he may harm the girl physically as I am quite sure he must have already tortured her mentally.

In that moment, Dr. Ranjan feels a profound heaviness, as if the weight of Kamal and Nanda's entire hellish existence has settled upon his shoulders. All his medical training, all his years of clinical practice - nothing can prepare him for the pitch-black abyss of depravity he now finds himself staring into.

He knows he shall turn back, withdraw from this mire before it can consume what remains of his own sanity. But somewhere amidst the darkness, a flicker of pity flickered to life. Nanda is alone in this pit of nightmare.

"Thank you for your courage in telling me this terrible truth," he says at last, his voice sounding far away even to his own ears. "I will do everything in my power to help Nanda escape her torment, no matter what it takes."

Shikha's lips curve in a bitter semblance of a smile. "Then you have more strength than I, doctor. For all our sakes...I pray you succeed."

As Dr. Ranjan departed back into the smothering night, her final whispered words trail after him, flaying what little hope he has left:

"Kamal Banerjee is no man...he is the very incarnation of evil itself. And that devil cannot be stopped once it takes root..."

CHAPTER TWELVE

Dr.Ranjan

I left Shikha's house with a confused and troubled mind. As per Shikha, Kamal displayed dual personalities. In such cases the victim doesn't know that he has another personality. He also remains unknown about the activities of the other one. According to Kamal's school teacher Nidhiram Saha, Kamal is possessed by demons because he has displayed different personalities since childhood.

Nanda also spotted Kamal on bed and in the kitchen at the same time. She is convinced that Kamal has demonic power. Now being a doctor, the 'demonic possession' theory seems obsolete to me. Seeing Kamal at different places at the same time must be hallucinations. So Mr.Nidhiram Saha and Nanda both had hallucinations which was very unlikely. Kamal had no twins. So practically none can see two Kamals at the same place at the same time.

On the other hand, villagers tagged Nanda as 'Pishachini' who sucked life out of her mother Bindu and friend Amaresh. Still educated people in villages believe in myths like 'Devil' or ' Demonic power`. They believe that showing multiple personalities is a trait of demonic possession. Under extreme mental pressure and stress people can start hallucinating.

In the case of Nanda, she lost her mother at birth. Unfortunately, her mother wanted to kill Nanda before birth inside her womb. She didn't want this child. A pregnant mother's mental trauma affects her baby's development in the long term. Nanda might have gone through extreme insecure and uncertain situations since her childhood. So her fear instigated her hallucination. But why was she afraid of Kamal? What was her fear about her husband? Kamal seems a caring and loving husband but if he possesses dual personalities, then his other personality may be the cause behind of Nanda`s fear. On the other hand, whatever Nanda's uncle Motilal Kundu told about Nanda's behaviour, was not clear. Most surprisingly Motilal also had the same verdict about Nanda's 'Demonic power'. He also thought that Nanda killed her mother Bindu. Being inside her womb, Nanda sucked out mother's life!

Even in the case of Amaresh also, Motilal held Nanda responsible. He never said anything in Nanda's defence. Motilal tried to convince me that he loved Nanda very dearly and Nanda was also very fond of him but Nanda never mentioned him in her story. Why did Nanda avoid taking her uncle's name?

Many doubts and confusions are standing in the way of clear analysis. Future of two lives depends now on me. Who is the predator and who is the victim? I have to find the answer.

I have to go back to village Maynapur and also to the town where Nanda's father used to practice homeopathy. It's really important to talk to Nanda's father, Rakesh Chatterjee. He may be able to shed light on the unsolved mystery

It's very tough to make time from my busy schedule at the clinic. Being a responsible doctor, I can't cancel appointments of all my patients. Nanda and Kamal have to wait a week more. Meanwhile I will wrap up with all ongoing cases.

CHAPTER THIRTEEN

Nanda

I'm trembling uncontrollably, my wrists and ankles chafing against the rough ropes binding me to bed. The musty air is suffocating me as I struggle to breathe through the filthy rag stuffed in my mouth. It's dark everywhere. Where am I? Why am I tied to a bed? Who is punishing me like this?

An old man's twisted face leers down at me, his yellowed teeth bared in a sadistic grin. "You murdered your own mother, you vile creature," he hisses, spittle flying from his lips. "You ate her from the inside out like a parasite."

I squeeze my eyes shut, trying to block out his words, but they bore into my mind like hot pokers. Sobs wrack my body as he continues his vicious tirade.

"You deserve no happiness, no love! You're an abomination that should have been snuffed out at birth!" He grips my chin with his gnarled, filthy hands, forcing me to look into his crazed eyes. "But don't worry, I'll make sure you're punished properly for your sins."

His hands release my face only to start tearing at my clothes. I writhe frantically, my muffled screams going unheeded as his repulsive body covers mine. Tears of terror and disgust stream down my cheeks as his violation begins anew.

No matter how hard I fight, how much I struggle, I'm powerless against this human monster. I've tried to end this nightmare so many times before, but he always comes back for me, his perverse cravings never satisfied. I have no voice, no escape from this living hell of torture and blame for sins I never committed.

I can only pray that one day, my personal demon will be exorcised and I can know peace. But tonight, I am his plaything to abuse as his sickened mind desires. Tonight, I remain trapped in darkness, trying not to drown amid the crashing waves of agony searing my very soul.

I'm gasping for air, my lungs burning as I finally manage to throw this creep off of me. He crashes against the wall, dazed for a split second - just enough time for me to wrench free of the ropes and scramble off the bed.

I run for the door, flinging it open and fleeing out into the night. The cool air slaps my face as I stumble down the dirt path, my bare feet slicing on rocks and twigs. I don't dare look back.

But then the angry voices reach my ears, carrying on the wind like the haunting whispers of the damned. I turn to see a mob of villagers emerging from their huts, faces twisted with hatred and revulsion.

"Devil's spawn!" an old woman screeches, hurling a rock that clips my shoulder. "You sucked the life out of poor Amaresh!"

The chants rise into a feverish crescendo. "Burn the witch! Burn her!"

I run blindly, desperately, as the horde pursues me like rabid dogs. Branches whip my face and arms as I plunge through the forest, but I can't stop. If they catch me...

My foot snags a twisted root and I go down hard, slamming into the unforgiving ground. I can hear them closing in, torchlight flickering through the trees. Scooping up a thick branch, I prepare to fight for my life.

But then my own scream ripping from my throat as I jolt awake, thrashing against my sweat-soaked sheets. It was just a nightmare, but one that felt terrifyingly real.

I draw my knees up, wrapping my trembling arms around them as I try to slow my ragged breathing. Even now, I can still hear the villagers' vicious taunts echoing endlessly in the shattered recesses of my mind.

How much more of this can I endure before I completely lose my grip on reality? I squeeze my eyes shut, rocking back and forth as I wrestle with the horrific visions. There has to be a way to end this torment, this unending onslaught of cruelty and pain.

Please, someone save me from this waking nightmare. I can't escape on my own.

****

Nanda is lying on the bed looking at the moving ceiling fan. She has been thinking if that fan can bear her body weight. Yes, she is planning to hang herself. The past few months have been unbearable for her. She is tired of her misfortune. She can't trust anyone in the world. She has nowhere to take shelter. She is feeling so lonely and helpless. Only meeting Dr. Ranjan has brought some hope.

But weeks have passed, there is no response from him. Has he given up on her? She has hinted about her miserable situation to him. But she is not sure if Dr. Ranjan can help her at all. Will he rescue Nanda from this living hell or let Nanda die slowly? Nanda can't find the right answer but she is eagerly waiting for one.

Few days later, Dr.Ranjan receives a call from Kamal. Kamal informs him that Nanda's condition has been worsening day by day. She needs to be admitted to a mental hospital soon. Dr.Ranjan assures Kamal that he will meet Nanda soon and start her treatment immediately.

Kamal unwillingly has agreed to wait for Dr.Ranjan to start treatment. Dr. Ranjan has realised that there is no time to waste. He has to meet Rakesh as soon as possible otherwise some unwanted situation may develop. It is a question of two lives. As planned, he leaves for the search of Nanda's father, Dr.Rakesh.

CHAPTER FOURTEEN

Batshala

My jeep's tires crunch on the dusty streets of Batshala as I make my way through the remote town near 'Maynapur' village. With each passing mile, it feels like I am being subsumed deeper into a waking nightmare from which there is no escape.

After the harrowing revelations about Kamal's depravity from Shikha, the rational part of my mind has screamed at me to cut my losses and return to Calcutta. Yet that flicker of determination or curiosity has compelled me to unearth every last detail of this disturbing case.

From the whispers and furtive glances of Batshala's locals, I gradually manage to gather the whereabouts of my next subject - Rakesh Chatterjee, Nanda's father and once a respected homeopathic practitioner in these parts. It seems the horrors surrounding his life had driven the man to exile himself from the town altogether some years ago.

The trail leads me to a secluded dwelling on the outskirts of Batshala. My consistent knocking on the creaky door is being unanswered for so long. I start to wonder if the dwelling is abandoned after all. Just as I prepare to give up, a tremulous voice comes from within.

"I have announced many times before that I am not to be disturbed at this time. Scoundrel Nepal you have come again to irritate me! I will kill you today!"

Drawing a steadying breath, I raise my voice. "Mr. Chatterjee? I mean you no harm or trouble, I assure you I am not Nepal. My name is Dr.Ranjan, and I've come regarding your daughter Nanda..."

A profound silence meets my words, stretching out into an eternity of its own. Then a hollow rasp: "That poor, forsaken child. So the curse truly refuses to die, even now."

The door creaks open and a middle-aged man`s face comes forward. "What devilry possesses you, doctor, to come dragging up such shame from the past? I want no part of it, I tell you!"

Steeling myself, I press on. "Your daughter is deathly ill, Mr. Chatterjee - not just physically, but her very sanity has been deeply scarred. As her husband's physician, I've come to understand the roots of her anguish in the hope I can help her escape this torment. For that, I need to know everything about her past, no matter how dark or painful."

Another ominous pause. Then, with a weary sigh, the door swings open and the wizened figure beckons me inside with a bony hand. "So be it, doctor. You've been warned about the shadows you'll be Made to confront."

I enter the house and sit on the chair, the only visible sitting arrangement in that small room. I find myself pinned by Chatterjee's haunted gaze, who sits on the bed folding his legs.

"You wish to know about Nanda, my daughter whom I never got a chance to know. But before that you must know of my Bindu's fate - Nandu's poor, sweet mother." His voice dropped to a hoarse rasp. "Then I must rip out my very heart to relive those memories once more..."

He falls silent for a long moment, some unnameable emotion contorting his features. He finally continues:

"Bindu was the most gentle, loving soul imaginable when I first knew her - more akin to a radiant goddess than a mere mortal woman. Even from our first meetings, her warmth and kindness shone out like a balm for this world's cruelties.

"But that inner light..." Chatterjee's eyes squeeze shut, glittering with unshed tears. "That light couldn't hope to endure against the black malignancy she was fated to become entangled with. Not when the foulest depths of human perversion are involved."

An icy trickle of dread trailed down my spine as the implications come into focus. Is Bindu`s past answer to Nanda`s present condition?

"She was so strong for so long, my brave Bindu. Keeping his foulest acts secret, even from me, just to preserve our child's safe life that while longer. All to delay the moment Nandu would inevitably become...engulfed..."

I watch in mute shock as thick tears began trailing down the hollows of Chatterjee's face, glimmering in the dim light like shards of glass.

"In the end, it wasn't the choking vines of that devil`s sadism that killed her." His voice drops to a broken whisper. "It was the shame over failing to protect her unborn little girl, to protect me. The self-hatred and despair flooded. After that, she simply subsided. Lost the will to keep drawing breath."

Reflexive nausea clenches my gut as the unvarnished tragedy washes over me. This poor, helpless woman inches from the grave yet still desperately shielding her unborn child in what little ways she could...until the last flickers of her selfhood were simply extinguished by the magnitude of her violation.

What psychic scars must such an incident have inflicted on the young Nanda's tender psyche? No wonder the woman teetered on the abyss of existential madness.

I become aware of Chatterjee observing me, eyes glinting with sadness.

My throat feels scalded as I force out the words: "You have to tell me everything. Every truth about Bindu. I cannot turn back now. Not when an innocent life still exists to be reclaimed from these depths of suffering. Nanda deserves to know even a fleeting taste of the peace your Bindu was denied."

Whether my declaration strikes a chord, or simply reveals the extent of his utter despair, I can't say. Chatterjee merely inclines his head in a skeletal nod.

"Then you are either the most courageous or foolhardy of men, doctor. For if my experience is any guide, you are already damning yourself to an eternity of night terrors from which you'll never escape..."

I think of poor, sweet Nanda adrift in that ink-black sea of torment from the cradle. I shudder anew and brace myself to hear the shameful, terrible past of Bindu.

Ithas been really a test of my expertise for many years. After meeting Nanda's father Rakesh, I have gotten replies to all my unanswered questions and also my confusions have received some clarification. At first, he had been really stubborn to say anything regarding Nanda.

Being a father is a great responsibility. Even Rakesh couldn't ignore it. He answered all my questions honestly. He agreed to come with me to Kamal's house to meet Nanda. I also requested Nanda's uncle Motilal Kundu and Kamal's teacher Nidhiram Saha to join us at Kamal's house.

All of them are going to play very important roles in revealing the mystery behind Nanda's weird behaviour and mental illness. I didn't inform Kamal about these guests who were going to accompany us in the meeting. I don't want his other personality to plan anything mischievous which can be harmful for Nanda.

****

One week has passed, Kamal is sitting on the balcony with a heavy heart. Gone are those days when he and Nanda both used to sit there and had their afternoon tea. Every day Nanda used to make some tasty snacks and they enjoyed eating together. But since that night's event Nanda has been keeping herself locked inside the bedroom most of the time.

For the past two months they have hardly talked to each other. Nanda has become more violent and hysterical. Kamal has decided to put Nanda in a mental asylum as soon as possible but he has to postpone the whole plan till Dr. Ranjan's next meeting. Hopefully the doctor will succeed to treat Nanda giving her some pill to forget about the past incidents. Nanda must not remember what happened. Otherwise, Nanda will have to go to a mental asylum- Kamal has made up his mind.

In the afternoon Kamal gets a call from Dr. Ranjan. He requests Kamal to arrange a meeting with Nanda. At that meeting he will treat Nanda. After that Nanda will recover fully. Kamal feels very excited hearing such good news. He eagerly awaits that day

CHAPTER FIFTEEN

Who is `The Other One`?

It is a Sunday afternoon. Dr. Ranjan has brought Motilal Kundu, Nidhiram Saha, Rakesh Chatterjee and also director of mental asylum Dr.Sudhangsu Haldar along with him. All of them are sitting in the front room at Kamal's house. Kamal seems quite uncomfortable in the presence of uninvited guests of that day.

"Dr. Ranjan, you have come to meet Nanda and treat her. Why did you bring all these people with you? Nanda is my wife and I don't want my wife's mental illness to become a topic of public discussion. I want my privacy. I don't want you to treat Nanda in front of all these people. Please tell them to leave immediately!" Kamal has lost his temper and become quite aggressive while talking to Dr. Ranjan.

Dr. Ranjan tries to calm him down and says, "Look Kamal, I can understand your worry about Nanda. To treat her we need to know the source of her mental stress. I believe these people can help us to do that. So please have patience and sit down. Let me do my work."

Nanda has been in her room since morning and refuses to open the door. Dr. Ranjan knocks at the door and calls out her name, "Nanda, I am Dr. Ranjan. I have come to remove all your fear from your mind. I brought your father also. He is very tensed about you. We all are here today to give you freedom from this darkness. For that you have to come out to the light. I know why you locked yourself inside. But now is the time you should come out and join us. I promise you that none can harm you anymore."

After a few minutes, Nanda opens the door. Her hands are shaking. She can hardly look up to anyone. Dr.Ranjan helps her to sit on a chair and hands her a glass of water. Since the last meeting Nanda has changed a lot. Her skin has turned pale and one can see bones under her skin. There is no smile on her face, only fear is dominating in her eyes. She is again uncomfortable at Kamal's presence but Dr.Ranjan helps her to calm down.

The dimly lit room is thick with tension as if the haunted eyes of Nanda meet those of her tormentors. Dr. Ranjan has assembled this twisted cast - the cunning uncle Motilal Kundu, Nanda's father Rakesh who has abandoned her, and worst of all, her own husband Kamal, the wolf she has unknowingly invited into her life.

Dr. Ranjan starts his speech addressing all, "We are here today not only to find a solution to the problems this couple have been facing for so long but also save them from further mental stress and agony. I have taken statements from both Nanda and Kamal. I have checked their backgrounds; talked to people who have known them for a long time. I have made my own analysis comprising all information and today I will like to tell you all a story based on my analysis. Let's start with Nanda."

Dr.Ranjan looks at Nanda with a smile of affection and continues, "Since birth Nanda has been always blamed for the death of her mother. Even her father left her when she was a mere baby. Her grandparents took care of her. Still she always felt deprived of motherly love and care. Nanda was a gorgeous little girl. In our society being a beautiful girl often becomes a curse. Same thing happened to Nanda. Nanda's uncle Motilal was quite fond of his niece but in a nasty way. Nanda was molested by her own uncle Motilal Kundu again and again at a very young age. She tried to tell about this but none believed her. Everyone in the family thought it's the 'Pishachini' inside her who was putting such dirty blame on her own uncle who claimed to love Nanda as his 'daughter'."

"What is this? Is this any kind of drama going on here? You are putting baseless blames on me Dr. Ranjan. Don't forget I have been a teacher in school for many years. I have a reputation and I won't let you destroy that. Stop playing such nasty games. If Nanda told you such things about me then you are just an idiot to believe her. It's all her drama! She is a cursed girl. The moment you give her entry in your life, your life gets destroyed!" Motilal Kundu starts shouting at Dr. Ranjan.

Dr. Ranjan raise his hand up and says, "Keep quiet Mr. Kundu. According to you all blames are baseless. Nanda told all lies to frame you, right?? Then listen to me very carefully. Nanda told me nothing about her childhood molestation because she didn't realise that she got molested. She thought she was getting punished because of the

'Pishachini' inside her. You were the person who put such an idea inside her brain for fulfilling your dirty desire. You would have continued molesting Nanda unless Nanda's father Rakesh caught you red handed. Am I right, Rakesh?" Dr.Ranjan turns towards Rakesh for his response.

Rakesh Chatterjee has been silently observing the whole situation. Now it is his turn to open up with his story that he earlier told Dr.Ranjan. Rakesh starts with a heavy heart, " I married Bindu against my parents' wish. We were

Brahmins and Bindu belonged to another caste. I shifted to town after marriage. I started my homeopathy practice. Whatever I earned was enough for our small family. We were happy together. After two years Bindu got pregnant with Nanda.

In the beginning, we were very happy and eagerly waiting to welcome the new guest in our life. As I kept busy the whole day, I couldn't take care of Bindu properly. One day Bindu's cousin brother Motilal came to our house. He insisted on taking Bindu with him back to the village where she would be taken care of properly. Bindu was not willing to go back. She kept on making excuses like if she left then there won't be anyone to cook for me, to make tea for me etc. But I didn't listen to such silly excuses, instead I sent her with Motilal forcefully.

After a few weeks, I received a letter from her. In that letter she requested to bring her back to town otherwise she threatened to kill herself. Being worried I boarded the next train available for Maynapur. Bindu was residing at his uncle's house there. Upon reaching I saw Bindu lying on the bed and crying profusely. I was really worried seeing Bindu's deteriorated health and disastrous mental condition. Motilal informed me that Bindu tried to kill her baby several times as she believed that evil was growing inside her womb.

I tried to calm down Bindu and make her understand that all she was thinking about the baby was her imagination. But Bindu reacted aggressively whenever I said anything to protect our child. Bindu's grandmother was also tensed about her condition. She happily welcomed me as she believed that only I could remove Bindu's superstition about our baby.

She wanted to tell me something but was uncomfortable when Motilal was around. In the evening, she sent Motilal to market for grocery shopping. She looked very hesitant to say anything to me but at last she gathered the courage to share her concern. She said, "Rakesh, whatever I am going to tell you now may shock you but this is nothing but true. I would have never disclosed this but Nanda's pathetic condition made me open up. Bindu's father was a drunkard. He left my daughter Malati when she was carrying Bindu. Since then, Bindu and Malati had been staying with us. My son and daughter in law were not happy with this arrangement. They used to curse Malati often. Malati was very soft minded. She couldn't take such mental pressure anymore and committed suicide. I was bringing up Bindu with all care and affection.

My grandson Motilal had been notorious and crooked since childhood. He is seven years older than Bindu. He used to touch Bindu inappropriately when she was a little girl. I tried to protest but my son and daughter in law always took their son innocently. They pointed out Bindu's beauty as her vice. Days passed, Motilal grew up to be a very aggressive brat. He was thrown out of school for taking drugs. Later he was sent to town for further education. There also he misbehaved with a lady teacher and he was rusticated from college.

After that Motilal came back to the village. He was immediately drawn to exceptionally beautiful Bindu. At first, he proposed to marry Bindu. None of us accepted this illicit affair. Bindu kept trying to avoid Motilal. I caught Motilal imposing himself on Bindu a few times. It was getting out of control and Motilal's parents sent him away again.

After Bindu's marriage, I thought Motilal would change his attitude towards her. When Motilal decided to bring pregnant Bindu back here, I didn't doubt anything. But Motilal had not changed a bit. He started talking dirty with Bindu. I saw him threatening her and hurting her physically. I have grown too old to protect her from monsters like Motilal. Such a situation during pregnancy is very harmful for Bindu. Please take her with you to town. Motilal will try to stop you but your right on Bindu is much more than his. Please don't tell him about our conversation otherwise he will kill me! If possible, leave on the first train from here next morning."

She pleaded to me with tears in her eyes. I was so shocked that I really didn't know what to say. I decided to leave with Bindu as soon as possible. The next morning when I asked Bindu to pack her luggage and leave with me, she blatantly denied! I tried to convince her in many ways to come with me but she was not ready to listen to me at all. She started cursing me for her condition and told me to leave. I was completely at a loss as I didn't know how to convince Bindu.

For a few days I tried continuously but she paid no heed. She stopped eating and vowed for fasting until and unless I leave. I had to return to town without Bindu. I still don't know why Bindu refused to come with me. She was the one who went to the village unwillingly. If I could bring her with me in town, I would never have to face today's situation. My wife`s and daughter's lives would have been saved." Rakesh breaks down and everyone can feel the pain in Rakesh's voice.

"I know the reason Mr.Rakesh. I know why your wife Bindu refused to come with you." Dr. Ranjan tries to calm Rakesh. He continues, "Motilal is very cunning. He could guess that his grandmother might tell everything about his mischievous character to Mr. Rakesh. He threatened Bindu that if she planned to leave with Mr. Rakesh, he would kill him. Bindu knew very well what Motilal was capable of. She got really scared for her husband Rakesh. So she put up with the drama and made Rakesh leave her behind.

Motilal kept harassing Bindu sexually. Even he threatened Bindu that if she gave birth to a girl, he would molest her too. Such mental pressure made Bindu lose her mental stability. She started thinking that it's better for her unborn child to die rather than be molested by Motilal. She tried to kill herself and her yet to be born baby several times. She also tried to convince people to believe that her child was Devil's and the child possessed demonic power so that others would help her kill the child.

She had gone through a terrible childhood because of Motilal. She didn't want that to happen to her child too. She preferred death to sexual molestation for her child. Her weak body and mind could not bear the labour pain. So she breathed her last before she could even see her daughter's face.

Rakesh came to take Nanda with him but Motilal blamed him for Bindu's death and refused to hand over Nanda to him. But Rakesh was not ready to leave Nanda with Motilal knowing his past history with Bindu. Rakesh's parents came forward to take all the responsibilities of Nanda. Motilal had to accept such an arrangement unwillingly. Rakesh felt relieved and left town tension free as Nanda was in best hands.

Few years passed after Bindu`s death. Motilal managed to get a school teacher post in the village. Coincidentally Nanda was also a student of the lower class of the same school. Motilal had been waiting for a chance to mingle with Nanda for a long time. He never got married but had many affairs. Being a teacher, he tried to come close to Nanda. He also started taking her tuition at home. Nanda was becoming very fond of Motilal. She was not aware of Motilal's nasty intentions behind his sweet nature.

Gradually Motilal started sexually molesting Nanda. He was putting the wrong idea in her mind that she was solely responsible for her mother's death and Motilal was punishing her for that. Nanda believed Motilal and she had to accept all 'punishment'. Motilal's ugly plan was successful until Nanda's childhood friend Amaresh saw him touching Nanda inappropriately.

Amaresh was about to tell everyone about Motilal's evil deed. Motilal got scared of being exposed. So he put the blame on Amaresh for smoking ganja in the classroom. Amaresh got rusticated and shifted to town. Again Nanda started facing sexual harassment. Nanda's subconscious mind started thinking of Amaresh as her saviour.

She started imagining Amaresh around her from time to time. She shared the theory of evil Amaresh to spread fear in Motilal's mind, holding the hope that Motilal would refrain from doing nasty stuff with her. Nanda always mentioned Amaresh's presence to Motilal to save herself. Motilal also stopped coming near to Nanda fearing Amaresh could take revenge by exposing him.

After Amaresh's untimely demise when everyone was blaming Nanda, she took it as an opportunity. She started behaving like a mentally unstable person and locked herself inside a room to get rid of Motilal. She was successful in her plan as Motilal stopped seeing her since then.

Nanda started living a normal life behind closed doors. She finished graduation in private. Unexpected death of her grandmother shook her life again. Grandfather couldn't bear such shock and decided to visit pilgrimages. He wanted to marry her off as soon as possible. Nanda preferred to arrange the marriage far from the village so that Motilal could never enter her life again.

Narayan Chatterjee got news about Kamal from some unknown source and took Nanda with him to Kamal's place. After a few days, Nanda's grandfather left and never came back. Kamal married Nanda and they had a happy life together. Suddenly Nanda started hallucinating and their personal relationship ruined because of Nanda's mental illness."

As Dr. Ranjan methodically lays bare the sordid history, it has become terrifyingly clear that Nanda had been a victim since birth. Her own uncle Motilal, a monster in human skin, has robbed her of her innocence at a tender age through horrific sexual abuse. The crimes he committed while arrogantly claiming to love her like a daughter, sickens all present.

Rakesh's voice has caught in his throat as he remembers how he had sent his pregnant wife Bindu away, straight into Motilal's lair of depravity. Bindu had tried to warn him, but sealed her own fate by refusing to leave, paralyzed by fear of what Motilal would do to Rakesh. She had died bringing Nanda into the world, haunted until the end by Motilal's vile threats to violate her daughter as he had her.

The look of anguish on Rakesh's face as he realized his failure to protect them cut straight to the soul. If only he had been stronger, braver, none of this would ever have happened.

Dr.Ranjan took a pause and again started," Now I would like to shed a light on Kamal's life . I met Kamal's teacher Mr. Nidhiram Saha in their village and got to know about Kamal's past life. I would like to request Mr. Nidhiram to correct me if I miss any point while narrating Kamal's story.

Kamal was the only son of a school teacher in Maynapur village. He was a brilliant boy with high scores in school examinations. But very few people knew about the crooked mind. Kamal told me about the story of his drowning in a river. But he told me the half truth. On that fateful day Kamal didn't go to the river with his friends for fishing but to tease the young girls who were taking bath there. When Kamal tried to pull the saree of one of the girls, all the girls got angry and attacked him. I got to know this truth by interrogating one of his childhood friends who accompanied Kamal on that eventful day.

So being chased by girls, Kamal went to deeper water to save himself. As he didn't know how to swim, he drowned. I guess that he didn't die but lost senses. His heart stopped beating for some time and people took him as dead. Few minutes later after being buried Kamal got his senses back. I heard Kamal's father had been at the burial site the whole night. Most probably he heard his son's cry and rescued him. But unfortunately, he is not alive amongst us for testimony.

Next day when the local people saw Kamal alive, they started believing the 'Demonic power' theory. Kamal used such superstition in his favour. He started acting weird to strengthen fear in people's minds. So that he could continue with his mischieves. His teacher Mr.Nidhiram caught him red handed smoking and drinking in the classroom many times.

To stop Mr. Nidhiram to complain against him, Kamal frightened him inside the forest on the way home. There were many people who witnessed Kamal's dark side but never dared to be open about it. Kamal had grown up to be a ruthless young man full of lust and greed for women. At first, he displayed his gentle, sober and kind Avatar. Later his dirty claws used to come out of the sleeves. He had several relationships but none could survive because of his flawed character.

After mother's death Kamal became more desperate to get married. He wanted to torture someone whole life with his lust not love. His marriage with Shikha Roy was almost final but he couldn't hide his real character for long. Shikha broke the engagement with Kamal.

When Mr. Narayan came to his house with a marriage proposal for his granddaughter Nanda, Kamal grabbed the opportunity immediately. Mr.Narayan might have come to know some character flaws of Kamal and wanted to check on them before the marriage. So he left a letter requesting Kamal to keep the marriage on hold until his return.

But Kamal was not ready to delay the marriage. He had the fear of being exposed. So he convinced Nanda that it was her grandfather's wish to marry her off as soon as possible. Nanda had to marry Kamal in absence of her grandfather. The first few days of marriage went off well as Kamal was in his best self. The animal inside him was yet to show its true self. Nanda started thinking that finally she was in safe hands. Eventually Kamal showed his brutal face to Nanda. He started raping her and if Nanda tried to protest, he used to beat her brutally."

"Lies! All are lies! "-Kamal protests. "Dr. Ranjan is a liar! He is trying to frame me. I have done nothing wrong with Nanda. She is my wife. I love her with all my heart. How can I even think of beating her. She had a nightmare. Since then, she had been acting weird. For her recovery I sought Dr. Ranjan's help. I am a responsible and caring husband. I don't know why the doctor is putting all the blame on me! I am the victim here. I thought finally I found my family with Nanda after marriage. But all my dreams for the future got shattered due to Nanda's illness. Now if you are unable to treat her, please don't blame me to hide your failure." Kamal shouts at Dr. Ranjan.

Dr. Ranjan laughs at Kamal and said, "Patience Kamal, patience. I never hold someone responsible without enough proof and proper hypothesis. If Nanda's grandfather really wanted to marry her off with you, it should have been mentioned in the letter. He requested you to wait for him to return. But you didn't wait for him because you knew that he went to gather information about you. If all these are lies, then show me the letter in front of everyone. I will accept my failure. I know you can't show that letter cause you must have destroyed it so that none could know that you married Nanda by cheating on her. Also I have a hunch that you also have threatened Narayan Chatterjee, Nanda's grandfather, to refrain from keeping any relationship with Nanda. Your neighbour Ms.Damini has confirmed that. She heard it all When you were terrorising that poor old man at your door step. Am I right Kamal?"

Kamal keeps silent, hanging his head. Dr. Ranjan continues, "Nanda fell into depression after being sexually assaulted by Kamal. In her mind she considered the image of Kamal who treated her lovingly for the first few days of marriage as her real husband. She had respect and love for her `husband`. But she hated the other image of Kamal who ill-treated her. In her mind this crooked Kamal is 'the other one' whom she despises and refuses to keep any relationship with.

Whenever Kamal used to be gentle and soft spoken, Nanda's subconscious mind imagined him as her real `husband`. Nanda's mental illness began with her imagination. Her protective subconscious made her hallucinate her loving husband around her. She started seeing two Kamals – one the loving man she married, her husband` and another the real Kamal, `The other one`. To protect herself Nanda takes shelter in her bedroom. She doesn't allow 'The other one' to harm her anymore."

Dr.Ranjan takes a break. There was pin drop silence in the room. It is now no secret that like a beast lying in wait, Kamal married Nanda under false pretenses, luring her into what seemed like a haven only to unleash his monstrously violent and abusive nature upon her. His pathetic denials and tantrums laid bare the dark cravings of a sociopath for power and gratification through tormenting the vulnerable.

The sickening layers of Nanda's torment have become known to all present. Each revelation is more horrific than the last. Dr. Ranjan's firm voice has commanded the room - a glimmer of reason and justice in a world gone insane. He surgically has exposed the manipulations and machinations through which evil has worked its way into this poor woman's life.

At last, he turns to Nanda, the broken porcelain doll before them. Dr.Ranjan walks towards Nanda. Nanda is still sitting on a chair with an emptiness in her eyes. She has not reacted even once in the whole conversation. His words flow like a cleansing river.

Dr. Ranjan continues, "Nanda didn't get mother's love and affection. She grew up with the burden of mother's death. She was even deprived of father's support. So she tried to find a father figure in her uncle Motilal but failed. Motilal took advantage of her innocence and molested her. Nanda couldn't share her pain and agony to anyone. She went through tremendous mental pressure. Even after marriage also she became victim of domestic violence and marital rape.

Many girls like Nanda are getting sexually abused since childhood without realising that they are being wronged. Most unfortunately, they fall victims to very near and dear ones like uncles, cousins. They have to keep their mouths shut to maintain their family's reputation unscathed. In this process, they start blaming themselves for what happened. Nanda is no different. Her mind could not take more when she found out about the true nature of her husband Kamal. She lost her mental balance. For her recovery, she needs mental support. She needs to feel safe. Mr. Rakesh, your only daughter needs you most. Only your love and affection can heal her wounded mind."

Mr. Rakesh holds Nanda's hands and says, "Ma Nanda, I have failed you as a father. I abandoned you when you needed me most. I will not beg your forgiveness but give me a chance to be your 'father'. I will not disappoint you this time. I will take you with me. You will study again and get a job. You will make decisions for your own life. Your father will always be with you. There will be no 'the other one' in your life".

Nanda looks at Rakesh. Tear drops rolled down Nanda's cheeks. He has given her the greatest gift - the truth about her worth, the assurance that the crimes against her are not her fault. She has no hand in her mother's death. She is never to endure any punishment. She is entitled to have a peaceful, happy life. The promise of a father's love from Rakesh to help her heal.

As Nanda's tears have flowed, it is as if an exorcism has begun. The demons of her past have been dragged into the light. Their foul mysteries have been dispelled by truth. Though the road ahead is long, she can begin to be free.

www.ingramcontent.com/pod-product-compliance
Lightning Source LLC
Chambersburg PA
CBHW031456150726
47990CB00007B/2784

9798894461106